THE BRUMBACK LIBRARY

OF VAN WERT COUNTY

VAN WERT, OHIO

THE DOG
THAT STOLE
FOOTBALL PLAYS

Books by Matt Christopher

Sports Stories

THE LUCKY BASEBALL BAT

BASEBALL PALS

BASKETBALL SPARKPLUG

TWO STRIKES ON JOHNNY

LITTLE LEFTY

TOUCHDOWN FOR TOMMY

LONG STRETCH AT FIRST
   BASE

BREAK FOR THE BASKET

CRACKERJACK HALFBACK

BASEBALL FLYHAWK

SINK IT, RUSTY

CATCHER WITH A GLASS
   ARM

TOO HOT TO HANDLE

THE COUNTERFEIT TACKLE

LONG SHOT FOR PAUL

THE TEAM THAT COULDN'T
   LOSE

THE YEAR MOM WON THE
   PENNANT

THE BASKET COUNTS

CATCH THAT PASS!

SHORTSTOP FROM TOKYO

LUCKY SEVEN

JOHNNY LONG LEGS

LOOK WHO'S PLAYING
   FIRST BASE

DIRT BIKE RACER

THE TWENTY-ONE-MILE
   SWIM

TOUGH TO TACKLE

THE KID WHO ONLY HIT
   HOMERS

FACE-OFF

MYSTERY COACH

ICE MAGIC

NO ARM IN LEFT FIELD

JINX GLOVE

FRONT COURT HEX

THE TEAM THAT STOPPED
   MOVING

GLUE FINGERS

THE PIGEON WITH THE
   TENNIS ELBOW

THE SUBMARINE PITCH

POWER PLAY

FOOTBALL FUGITIVE

THE DIAMOND CHAMPS

JOHNNY NO HIT

THE FOX STEALS HOME

SOCCER HALFBACK

JACKRABBIT GOALIE

THE DOG THAT STOLE
   FOOTBALL PLAYS

Animal Stories

DESPERATE SEARCH

STRANDED

EARTHQUAKE

DEVIL PONY

THE DOG
THAT STOLE
FOOTBALL PLAYS

BY
MATT CHRISTOPHER

Illustrated by Bill Ogden

Little, Brown and Company
Boston   Toronto

j

FIRST EDITION

Library of Congress Cataloging in Publication Data

Christopher, Matthew F
  The dog that stole football plays

  SUMMARY: A boy and his dog are able to steal plays from the opposing football team.
  [1. Dogs—Fiction.   2. Extrasensory perception— Fiction.   3. Football—Fiction] I. Ogden, William, fl. 1972–   II. Title.
PZ7.C458Do   [Fic]   79-13266
ISBN 0-316-13978-5

BP

Published simultaneously in Canada by Little, Brown & Company (Canada) Limited

PRINTED IN THE UNITED STATES OF AMERICA

To Nicole

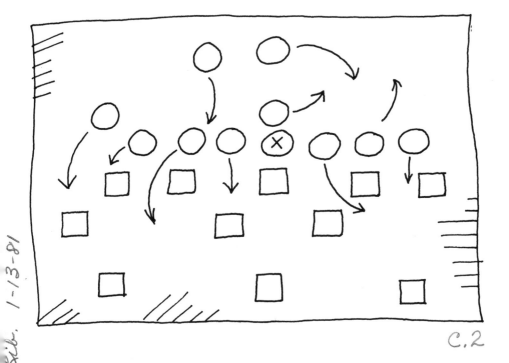

C.2

The dog was in the window of Pete's Pet Shop. He was an Airedale, with gray fur and white whiskers.

I'M HARRY, said the sign that hung from his neck.

"Hi, Harry," smiled Mike.

"Well, hi, kid! It's about time."

Mike stared. Had he really heard what he thought he had? The dog opened its mouth and licked its chops.

"Did — did you say that?" said Mike.

"I sure did," said Harry the dog. "I've been trying to tune in to some kid's mind ever since I've been cooped up in here."

"You — you mean that you can read my mind?"

Harry barked. "Wuff! And send my thoughts into your head, too. It's just a gift I've got. Hey, we seem to be a team.

How about buying me? I'm only twenty bucks. You can raise twenty bucks, can't you?"

Mike didn't know what to think. He couldn't believe he had met a dog who could read his mind. And to think that the dog could send him mental signals, too. It was — well, it was crazy.

But super!

There was only one trouble. He didn't have much money.

"Gee, Harry," said Mike. "I'd sure like to buy you. But I haven't got twenty bucks."

"Tell your father you've found a dog that can do handstands, roll over, and wiggle his ears," said Harry. "That gets 'em every time. Tell him you've got to own me. But don't tell him we can read

each other's minds. That's a secret just between you and me."

"OK," said Mike.

He started to leave, then thought of something.

"No," said Harry, reading his mind again. "I can't talk with any other human. Most dogs, yes. And a few cats, but you're the only kid I've been able to tune my mind in on."

"Do you have any brothers and sisters like you?" asked Mike.

"No. I'm the only one."

"I'll be back," Mike promised. "That is, I hope I will."

"Good luck," said Harry. "Hey! What's your name?"

"Mike," said Mike.

He ran all the way home and told his mother and father about Harry. He said he'd like to buy him, but Harry cost twenty dollars.

They seemed undecided, so he said Harry could do handstands, roll over and wiggle his ears, and that twenty bucks was dirt cheap for a dog like him.

His mother thought about it for a minute. "It's OK with me if it's OK with your father," she said.

"It's OK with me if you promise you'll
clean up after him," his father said.
"I promise, Dad!" said Mike happily.

The days after Mike bought Harry were very busy. Mike began school, and every day he went to football practice.

Then one evening Mike heard Harry say, "Hey, Mike, when are you going to take me to a practice or a game?"

"Harry, you'd just be in the way," Mike said. "And somebody might run out of bounds and step on you."

"No one will step on me," Harry answered. "And besides, I get tired of hanging around the house all by myself every afternoon. Even talking dogs like to play a bit. And you'll be surprised to find out how much I can help you."

Mike didn't think Harry would be any help at all, but he didn't want him to be lonely, so he brought him to the first game of the year.

Mike's team was the Jets, and they were playing the Rams, who had won the championship last year. Mike hoped his team would do well.

When the teams took the field, Harry stayed on the sidelines. Soon he managed to seat himself near the Rams' bench. He cocked his ears and began to listen very hard.

He soon discovered that the Rams'
coach sent instructions to the team on
every important play.

"Jones, take the ball, and go over left
tackle," he heard the coach say.

"Mike, watch for Jones going over left tackle," Harry thought.

On the field, Mike could scarcely believe what his dog had told him, but he ran up from his linebacker's slot and made the tackle. The Rams didn't gain a yard.

"Yeah, Mike!" the fans cheered.

The game went on, and thanks to Harry, the Rams hardly moved the ball at all. At the end of the first half, the score was Rams 0, Jets 0.

During the third quarter the Rams moved the ball to the Jets' twenty-eight-yard line. The situation was tense.

"What're you waiting for, Mike?" Butch said in the defensive huddle.

"Hold it!" said Mike.

The message was coming from Harry into his thoughts. "Thirty-two. Run through right tackle."

Mike smiled. "OK, guys! A run through right tackle! Cover that hole!"

Sure enough, the Rams' halfback tried

to bust through his right-tackle side, but
he didn't gain an inch. He *lost* a yard.

"Nice going, Mike!" cried Butch. "Good guess!"

The message from Harry came again. "Fourteen! Long pass down the right corner."

Mike looked at Butch. "Watch for a long pass down in your corner, Butch," he said.

Butch not only looked for it, but intercepted it, and carried it to the Rams' eighteen-yard line! In two plays they scored a touchdown; then they made the point after.

"Hey, you've guessed them right again, Mike!" exclaimed Bobby, a half-back. "That's great, man!"

Mike didn't tell him that it was really Harry who deserved all the credit.

24

The Jets won the game, 28 to 7.

The next week they played the Aces and beat them 14 to 0. Harry was making all the difference. But as he was walking home from the Aces game, Mike wondered briefly if using Harry were really a fair thing to do. It helped the Jets win, and that's what counted, wasn't it?

"We're really not cheating, are we, Harry?" Mike asked. "After all, anything to win, right, pal?"

Harry only gave a short bark and walked away. "Don't ask me. I'm just a dog. But anytime you don't want to hear the plays, it's all right with me." Mike decided it was too complicated to think about.

After their fourth win, Mike's father invited the Jets to Bailor's Chunky Hamburgers and bought them each a burger. While they ate, a tall kid with curly red hair came up to Mike and stuck a finger against his chest.

"You think you've got a great team, don't you?" he said, tough-like.

"Sure we do," agreed Mike. The kid was Curly Lucas, captain of the Tigers.

"We're playing you guys next week," said Curly. "How about the losers buying the winners hamburgers?"

"Sounds great," exclaimed Mike.
"Wait a minute. I'll talk to my father."

His father was sitting on the end stool.
Mike told him Curly's offer, and said, "I
think we can beat them, Dad."

"OK," said his father.

Mike wasn't worried. With Harry giving him the plays, the Jets would give the Tigers a drubbing they wouldn't forget.

But on Saturday morning, something happened that Mike had not counted on. Harry would not budge out of his house.

He was sick!

"It must have been that old bone I found in the yard," Harry groaned. "I just can't make it today."

"Oh, no!" cried Mike. And for a minute he thought he was going to get sick, too.

But the game had to go on — with or without Harry.

The Tigers were a fired-up ball team. They scored a touchdown within the first five minutes of the game.

The Jets' defense was full of holes, and
the Tigers seemed to know exactly
where every one of them was.

Mike saw Curly's triumphant smile,
and could picture him already munching
on the hamburg he was going to win.

Before the quarter ended, the Tigers had chalked up seven more points, 14–0.

Mike and his defensemen stood on the field, their spirits broken.

"You were crazy to take Curly up on that bet," Butch said, glaring at Mike. "Those Tigers are just too big for us, and your magic — or whatever it is — isn't working."

"I'm sorry," said Mike. "I'm really sorry about this."

He couldn't tell Butch that he had depended on his dog, Harry, to help them out. Why did that dumb dog have to get sick *now* of all times?

The Tigers went into the lead in the second quarter, 21–0.

At halftime Mike sat on the bench with his head in his hands.

Mike's father came over to the bench. "What are you doing?" he asked. "Giving up? If every guy had that attitude, our whole country would be in a lousy mess, not only our football team."

"But, Dad!" cried Mike. "We're not getting anywhere! They're bigger than we are!"

"So what? Whittle them down to your size," said his father.

Mike thought about that a minute. "You're right, Dad," he said. "They're bigger than we are, but if we give them a good fight —"

"You'll make it look more like a ball game," said his father.

Mike leaped off the bench, his heart suddenly filled with new hope.

"Hey, guys!" he cried. "Let's give those Tigers a fight the next half! Let's show them we're more than small guys! Let's show them we've got guts! OK!"

When the second half started, Mike said to himself, *We're going to win without Harry. We are. We are.*

They played like a changed team.

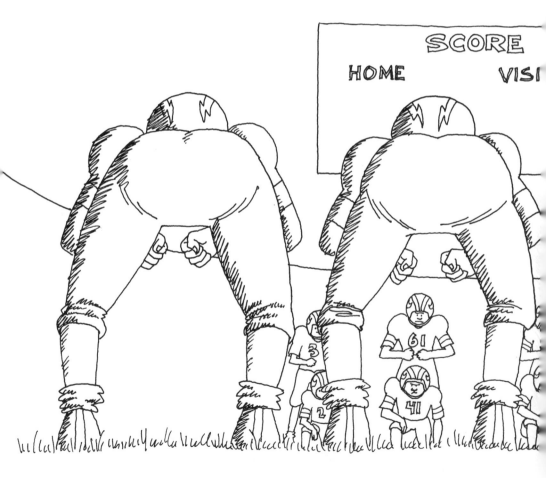

They ran harder. They tackled better.
They blocked. They knocked down
passes. Soon they were only one touchdown behind. With only three minutes
to go, Butch looked to the sidelines and

shouted, "Mike, look who just came into the park. Your dog, Harry! Maybe he'll bring us good luck."

Mike's heart leaped. "Oh, good, he's well!" he cried. "But we're doing all right without him."

"What?" said Butch, staring at him.

"We're not going to depend on Harry anymore, that's what," Mike replied. "We're going to play without his help."

Mike sent a message to Harry to keep quiet for the rest of the game and then yelled, "Let's go, guys!"

The Jets continued to play tough ball, and scored another touchdown. When the final whistle blew, the game was a tie, 21–21.

At the hamburger joint, the Jets and
the Tigers each bought a big hamburger.
But Mike bought an extra.

"Here," he said, giving it to Harry.
"This is a special award for you."

"Special award?" echoed Butch. "What did he do?"

Mike smiled. "He stayed home when we needed him the most."

His teammates looked at him curiously.

"He's been talking funny like that through the whole game," said Butch.

"So would you," said Mike, "if you had a dog like Harry. Right, Harry?"

"Wuff!" said Harry.